This book belongs to:

_____

_____

_____

First published 2000 by Walker Books Ltd
87 Vauxhall Walk, London SE11 5HJ

This edition published 2011

2 4 6 8 10 9 7 5 3 1

© 2000 Lucy Cousins
Lucy Cousins font © 2000 Lucy Cousins

"Maisy" Audio Visual Series produced by King Rollo Films for
Universal Pictures International Visual Programming

Maisy™. Maisy is a registered trademark of Walker Books Ltd, London.

The moral right of the author/illustrator has been asserted

Printed in China

All rights reserved

British Library Cataloguing in Publication Data:
a catalogue record for this book is available from the British Library

ISBN 978-1-4063-3481-4

www.walker.co.uk
www.maisyfun.co.uk

Maisy Goes Shopping

Lucy Cousins

WALKER BOOKS
AND SUBSIDIARIES
LONDON · BOSTON · SYDNEY · AUCKLAND

Maisy is visiting Charley today.

Hello, Charley.

Hello, Maisy.

It's nearly lunchtime, but Charley's fridge is empty.

It's time to go shopping!

Maisy chooses some apples and bananas.

Mmm, they look delicious, Maisy.

Charley gets some juice.

What else does he need?

Bread, tomatoes, cheese and yogurt – there, that's everything.

Now it's time to pay at the checkout.

Look at all that shopping!

It's lucky you brought your trailer, Maisy.

Maisy and Charley unpack the bags.

Then at last it's time to sit down ...

and have some lunch.
Hooray!

Read and enjoy the Maisy story books

Available from all good booksellers

It's more fun with Maisy!